PUFFIN BOOKS

Ursula Bear

Sheila Lavelle was born in Gateshead, County Durham, in 1939. When she was a child she spent all her time reading anything she could get her hands on and from the age of ten began to write plays, stories and poetry.

She married in 1958 and had two sons. When her children started school she returned to the writing that had been put on hold and sold some stories to a magazine. At the same time she trained as a teacher and taught in infant schools for ten years. Sheila Lavelle gave up teaching in 1976 to write full time. Her first book, *Ursula Bear*, was published in 1977.

Sheila Lavelle now lives in a cottage near the sea in Galloway, Scotland, with her husband and two border collies. She is now also a grandmother! Her days are spent writing in the morning and walking her dogs in the afternoon.

Some other books by Sheila Lavelle

FETCH THE SLIPPER
HARRY'S AUNT

For older readers

CALAMITY WITH THE FIEND
MY BEST FIEND
THE FIEND NEXT DOOR
TROUBLE WITH THE FIEND
REVENGE OF THE FIEND

SHEILA LAVELLE

Ursula Bear

Illustrated by Thelma Lambert

PUFFIN BOOKS

PUFFIN BOOKS

Published by the Penguin Group
Penguin Books Ltd, 27 Wrights Lane, London W8 5TZ, England
Penguin Putnam Inc., 375 Hudson Street, New York, New York 10014, USA
Penguin Books Australia Ltd, Ringwood, Victoria, Australia
Penguin Books Canada Ltd, 10 Alcorn Avenue, Toronto,
Ontario, Canada M4V 3B2
Penguin Books (NZ) Ltd, Private Bag 102902, NSMC, Auckland, New Zealand

On the World Wide Web at: www.penguin.com

Penguin Books Ltd, Registered Offices: Harmondsworth,
Middlesex, England

Ursula Bear first published by Hamish Hamilton Ltd 1977
Ursula Swimming first published by Hamish Hamilton Ltd 1990
Published in one volume in Puffin Books 1994
9 10 8

Text copyright © Sheila Lavelle, 1977, 1990
Illustrations copyright © Thelma Lambert, 1977, 1990
All rights reserved

The moral right of the author (and illustrator) has been asserted

Set in 15pt Baskerville by Rowland Phototypesetting Ltd
Bury St Edmunds, Suffolk

Made and printed in England by Clays Ltd, St Ives plc

British Library Cataloguing in Publication Data
A CIP catalogue record for this book is available from
the British Library

ISBN 0–140–36467–6

Ursula Bear

Ursula was a little girl who liked
bears. She liked big bears, small
bears and middle-sized bears. She
liked fat bears and thin bears.
She liked tall bears and short bears.
She liked furry bears and bare bears.
  She liked the live bears in the zoo,
the brown bears, the black bears, the
koala bears, the honey bears, the

5

polar bears and the grizzly bears.
She liked toy bears and teddy bears.
Her favourite toy was an old teddy
with no fur left called Fredbear. She
only liked boys if they were called
Rupert.

Ursula liked bears so much that
she wanted to be one.

Ursula lived with her Aunt
Prudence. One day she asked her

aunt, "How can I change into a bear?"

Aunt Prudence laughed. "Ursula, you are a silly little girl. Why do you want to be a bear? I like you just as you are."

But Ursula still wanted to be a bear.

One day, when she was alone in the house, Ursula got out Aunt Prudence's big brown fur coat and put it on. It was so long that it trailed on the floor and the sleeves hung down to the ground.

Ursula crawled all over the house, grunting and growling. It was lovely to pretend to be a bear.

But what Ursula wanted most of all was to be a real bear.

She went to the zoo and asked the big brown bear, "How can I turn into a bear?"

But he only growled and went on eating his bun.

Ursula liked books about bears. She liked Winnie the Pooh and Paddington and Teddy Robinson. She liked them even better than the Wombles. Her favourite story was "Goldilocks and the Three Bears" and she read it to Fredbear every night before they went to sleep.

One night she asked Fredbear, "How can I change into a bear?"

But he only looked at her with his one glass eye and said nothing.

At school one day Ursula had a good idea.

"I'll ask my teacher," she said.
"My teacher is sure to know because
teachers know everything."

Ursula's teacher didn't laugh. She
knew that it was a very important
question. But even she did not really
know the answer.

"Perhaps you could try to think

like a bear and act like a bear," she suggested. "And you could try eating all the things that bears like to eat."

Ursula thanked her and went home. There were beefburgers and chips for tea but Ursula didn't want any.

"Can I have some porridge for tea, please," she asked Aunt Prudence. "And some honey? And some

currant buns?" She knew there was no point in asking for eucalyptus leaves.

Every day for a week Ursula ate nothing but porridge and honey and currant buns. Every day for a week she looked in the mirror as soon as she woke up. But all she saw was the same pink face and brown curls and blue eyes.

On Saturday she went to the library. In the library she found a book about magic spells. On page one hundred and sixty-three it said, "How a little girl can turn into a bear."

Ursula closed her eyes tight. Then she opened them and looked again. It was true. That's just what it said

on page one hundred and sixty-three.
"How a little girl can turn into a
bear."

Ursula asked the librarian for a

piece of paper and a pencil. She copied down the spell.

"Two tablespoons porridge, one tablespoon honey, one large currant bun. Stir porridge and honey together and make into sandwich with currant bun. Recite these magic words while eating bun. I'M A BEAR, I'M A BEAR, I'M A BEAR, I'M A BEAR, I'M A BEAR, I'M A BEAR. To change back into a little girl again . . ."

But Ursula did not bother to read the rest. She ran all the way home, clutching her piece of paper tightly in her hand. She had been eating all the right things, but they hadn't worked without the magic words. Now she knew what to do.

When Ursula got home her Aunt Prudence had a visitor. It was Mrs Vickers from down the street. Ursula had once written a funny poem about Mrs Vickers but Aunt Prudence had said it was rude and had torn it up. Aunt Prudence and Mrs Vickers were sitting in the living-room together having a nice cup of tea and a cosy chat about Mrs Vickers' next-door neighbour who painted pictures and played the flute when she should have been doing the housework.

Ursula let herself in at the back door and went into the kitchen. She took out a small bowl and carefully mixed together two tablespoons of porridge and one tablespoon of honey. She stood on a chair to get a

currant bun out of the bread bin. She
cut the bun in half and filled it with
the porridge mixture. Then she put it
into a paper bag.

Very quietly she opened the back
door and went down the garden path
to the shed. There was a pile of clean
sacks in the corner and Ursula made
herself a comfortable seat and settled
down to eat her bun.

It took her a long time to finish it
for it was rather large and rather
sticky and she had to keep saying
"I'M A BEAR, I'M A BEAR, I'M A
BEAR," with her mouth full. But at
last she managed to swallow the last
bite. She licked her fingers clean and
waited to see what would happen.

Nothing happened. Exactly
nothing. Nothing at all. Ursula
became so fed up with waiting to
turn into a bear that at last she fell
asleep on the heap of sacks.

When she awoke it was beginning
to get dark and she knew it must be
nearly teatime. She hurried to the
house, but when she tried to open the

back door she found she could not reach the handle.

"That's funny," she thought. "I could reach it when I went out. Somebody must have moved it higher up."

She went round to the front of the house to knock on the front door.

Aunt Prudence was just showing her visitor out as Ursula came round the corner of the house. Both ladies shrieked when they saw Ursula, and slammed the door in her face.

Ursula stared at the door. She looked behind her to see if there was anything which could have frightened them. There was nothing there. Whatever could be the matter with them?

She bent down to shout through the letter-box, "Auntie, open the door. It's me, Ursula."

But no words came out of Ursula's mouth. Only a strange low grunting and growling noise.

"Whatever is the matter with my voice?" she thought. "I must have caught a cold from falling asleep in the shed."

Ursula put her ear to the letter-box to hear what was happening in the house. Aunt Prudence was talking on the telephone in the hall and she sounded very worried.

"Yes, sergeant, a bear," she was saying. "No, quite a small bear. But definitely a bear. And it looks quite fierce. It's trying to get into the house. And it's been growling through the letter-box."

Ursula went and stared through the French window of the living-room. Mrs Vickers was inside looking very white-faced and biting her nails. Ursula banged on the window and waved to her, but Mrs Vickers screamed and ran out of the room.

All at once Ursula noticed her own reflection in the glass of the window.

She saw a round furry face with a black snout and two round furry ears.

She saw a fat brown furry tummy and four brown furry paws.

She saw two black twinkling eyes. She stared and stared.

"That's me!" she growled at last. "I'M A BEAR!"

Ursula turned cartwheels all over the front lawn. She growled ferociously through the letter-box for two whole minutes. She scampered madly backwards and forwards along the path. She jumped up and down and stood on her head. Finally she lay on her back and waved her four furry feet in the air.

Suddenly she heard a loud wailing

noise and a white car pulled up at
the gate with a flashing blue light on
top and a siren blaring loudly.

"Police!" said Ursula to herself.
She scrambled quickly up the apple-
tree and hid in the topmost branches.

23

She peeped down through the leaves and saw two policemen walking up the path with sticks and nets. One of them was holding a torch and the other was carrying a gun. A GUN!

Ursula swallowed hard.

"Golly!" she thought. "I'd better find a safer hiding place than this."

One of the policemen knocked at the front door and Aunt Prudence let them in. As soon as they had disappeared inside, Ursula climbed down from the tree and darted across the road and down the street.

Mrs Vickers' next-door neighbour was called Mrs Martinez. She was different from the other people in the street because she was Spanish, and because she was an artist. She had a

very untidy house, and a garage
filled with paintings and old
canvasses and tubes of paint and
brushes and junk.

It was a good place to hide. Ursula
curled herself up in the darkest
corner of the garage and made
herself as small as possible, which
was quite small as the spell had
somehow made her shrink. She could
hear the policemen searching her
garden and she saw the torch flash
once or twice. But nobody came near
her hiding place.

At last the police car went away
and the street was quiet once more.
By now it was quite dark and Ursula
was feeling cold and hungry. But
what could she do? She could not go

home. She gave a sad little whimper when she thought about a hot supper and her nice warm bed. And how worried Aunt Prudence must be!

"I'd better turn myself back into a little girl again," she said to herself. "It wasn't such a good idea to be a bear, after all."

But poor Ursula had no idea

HOW to turn herself back into a little girl again. She hadn't read the second part of the spell.

Suddenly the light was switched on in the garage and Mrs Martinez came in. She began to rummage about among the boxes of paints, singing to herself, under her breath. She had a very kind face, and Ursula was so cold and hungry and miserable that she decided to take the risk. She crept out from the corner and put a furry paw on Mrs Martinez' leg.

Mrs Martinez jumped, but she didn't scream.

"Good heavens!" she cried. "A little bear. How sweet! How did you get in here?"

She picked Ursula up in her arms. "You must be berry cold, my poor little one. You are shibbering. I will gib you something to make you nice and warm."

Mrs Martinez could not say the letter 'V'. She always said 'B' instead. That was another reason why Mrs Vickers did not like her very much.

She carried Ursula into the house and put her on a rug in front of the fire.

"You have beautiful soft fur, little bear," she said. "It is like belbet!" She went out to the kitchen and

came back a few minutes later with a
steaming bowl of porridge. Ursula
ate every scrap and it was delicious.
Then Mrs Martinez put a soft
blanket into an old dog-basket and
tucked her up for the night.

Ursula was so worn out after all
her adventures that she went straight
to sleep.

Next morning, while Mrs
Martinez was making breakfast,

Ursula looked out of the window at her own house. The police were there again, and Ursula felt ashamed. She knew Aunt Prudence must be terribly worried about her.

After breakfast she took Mrs Martinez' hand and started to pull her towards the door.

"You want to go somewhere?" asked Mrs Martinez. "You want me to go weeth you?"

Ursula nodded her head as hard as she could and tugged at Mrs Martinez' hand.

"One moment, little one," said Mrs Martinez. "It is not good going like that. Somebody will put you in the zoo!"

She dressed Ursula in an old red

jumper which came down almost to her feet. She stuck her hind paws into an old pair of Wellingtons so that they didn't show. Finally she tied a shawl round her head and under her chin.

"Now, that's better," said Mrs Martinez. "You are little girl now, not little bear." And Mrs Martinez laughed merrily, thinking that she had made a very funny joke.

Ursula found it very difficult to walk in the Wellingtons, which were far too big for her. In the end Mrs Martinez had to pick her up and carry her. Ursula kept pointing her paw in the direction she wanted to go, and it was not long before they reached the library.

But it was Sunday. And of course the library was closed. And to make it worse the sign on the door said "Closed all day Sunday AND MONDAY".

Two big tears trickled down Ursula's brown furry cheeks.

"Don't worry, little one," said Mrs

Martinez. "I have hundreds of books at home. If you want books, I can gib you books, no?"

For most of that Sunday morning Ursula sat in the basket in front of the fire in Mrs Martinez' living room. All around her were huge piles of books. Kind Mrs Martinez kept bringing armfuls from the garage and

from the loft and she kept trying to make Ursula look at them.

"Look at this beautiful one. It has pictures of bears, just like you. What about this one with flowers and birds? You don't like any ob them, no?"

Ursula could only shake her head sadly. They were very nice books, but there was only one book she really wanted.

At last Mrs Martinez knelt on the floor and looked into Ursula's eyes.

"These are not the right books, no?"

Ursula shook her head.

"There is a special book you want, yes?"

Ursula nodded.

"And it is in the library, yes?"

Ursula nodded again.

"I see," said Mrs Martinez. "Now, is it very important that you have it today?"

This time Ursula nodded harder than ever.

"Well, I will see what I can do," said Mrs Martinez.

She patted Ursula's head and went out of the room. Ursula heard her making a telephone call in the hall. When she came back she was smiling.

"Now everything will be all right," she said. "My friend, Mr Blomeyer, is going to help us. He is a kind man, you will like him. Also he is on the Town Council and he has a key to the library."

Mrs Martinez dressed Ursula once more in her strange disguise. She was just tying the scarf under Ursula's chin when the doorbell rang.

"Great Scott!" said Mr Blomeyer

when he came into the room. "Is THAT the friend you were telling me about? What is this? A circus or something?"

"Now, now, Paul," said Mrs Martinez. "Don't be cross. You did promise to help, and it will only take a few minutes. And afterwards I will gib you nice lunch, no?"

"Nice lunch, yes!" said Mr Blomeyer and drove them to the library in his car. He opened the big oak door with one of a huge bunch of keys.

As soon as they were inside Ursula scampered to the shelf where she had found the book of spells. She recognised the book's blue and gold binding at once, but it was very

heavy and she had to wait for Mr
Blomeyer to lift it down for her and
put it on a table.

Mrs Martinez and Mr Blomeyer watched in amazement as Ursula scrabbled through the pages with her big hairy paws. It did not take long, because she remembered the page number. It was page one hundred and sixty-three. Ursula found the right page and pointed her paw at the title. "How a little girl can turn into a bear." She looked up at Mrs Martinez and Mr Blomeyer and then pointed to herself.

Mr Blomeyer and Mrs Martinez looked at Ursula. They looked at the book. They looked at one another. Then they looked at Ursula again. Their eyes grew round in astonishment.

"I don't believe it," muttered Mr

Blomeyer. "It can't be true. I just don't believe it."

Mrs Martinez just gazed into space and said nothing.

Ursula took no notice of either of

them. She was busy reading the second part of the spell.

"To turn back into a little girl again, eat a large plateful of beefburgers and chips and say "RAEB A M'I, RAEB A M'I, RAEB A M'I, RAEB A M'I, RAEB A M'I, RAEB A M'I." Which is, of course, I'M A BEAR backwards.

Ursula hugged both her friends in delight. She pointed again to the spell so that Mrs Martinez would read it.

Mrs Martinez still looked dazed, but she nodded her head.

"I understand," she said. "You want to go home now, no? And you want beefburgers and chips for lunch, yes?"

They all had beefburgers and chips for lunch, although Mr Blomeyer and Mrs Martinez could hardly eat theirs for staring at Ursula.

"RAEB A M'I," said Ursula, as she ate. "RAEB A M'I, RAEB A M'I." At least, that is what she meant to say. But as she could not speak, and could only growl, it didn't sound a bit like that at all. In any

case it was difficult to say anything
at all with her mouth full of
beefburger and chips and tomato
sauce and bread and butter, but
Ursula did her best.

Mrs Martinez and Mr Blomeyer
kept on staring at Ursula but of
course at first nothing happened. So
Ursula curled herself up on the sofa
and had a little nap.

And when she woke up there she
was in her blue cotton dress with her
pink face and her brown curls!

Her two friends were so amazed that they could hardly speak. Ursula quickly explained how it had all happened.

"I must go home at once," she told them. "Aunt Prudence will be so worried. And I don't know how I'm going to explain where I've been all night. If I tell her the truth she'll never believe me."

Mr Blomeyer scratched his head. "I think I can help you there," he said. "Supposing I took you home and said I had found you in the

library? You could have fallen asleep in a dark corner and got locked in by mistake when the library closed for the night. Then when I called at the library to do some of my paper work this afternoon I found you and brought you home."

And that is just what they did. Mr Blomeyer popped Ursula into his car

and drove a few yards down the street to her own house.

Aunt Prudence was so delighted to see Ursula safe and well that she completely forgot to be cross.

"You must be starving after being locked up all night with nothing to eat or drink," she said. "You just sit by the fire, Ursula dear, and I'll make you your favourite tea."

And she brought Ursula a tray piled high with . . .

Can you guess?

Yes.

Porridge. And honey. And currant buns.

Ursula
Swimming

Chapter One

Ursula woke up early one Saturday morning and looked at the blue summer sky.

"Who wants to come for a picnic by the river?" she said to her sixteen teddy bears.

The bears all gazed into space and said nothing. Even Fredbear, Ursula's favourite, went on staring at the wall.

"You're all a lot of lazy-bones," said Ursula. She pulled on her shorts and T-shirt and ran downstairs.

Ursula lived with her Aunt Prudence. She found her aunt in the kitchen, making pancakes for breakfast, and singing *The sun has got his hat on*, at the top of her voice.

"Hip hip hip hurray!" sang Ursula, joining in the song.

Aunt Prudence flipped the pancake over and caught it in the pan. "You sound happy today," she said.

"I am happy," said Ursula. "The sun's shining, there are pancakes for breakfast, it's Saturday and there's no school." She put her arms round her aunt's waist. "Can I have a picnic by the river, Aunt Prudence, please?"

"We'll see," said Aunt Prudence. "I've got a lovely surprise for you first."

Ursula sat down at the kitchen table. She knew it must be something nice by the big smile on her aunt's face.

Then Ursula noticed that four places had been laid at the table. She stared in astonishment.

"Who's coming for breakfast?" she said.

"That's the surprise," said Aunt Prudence. She tipped the pancake onto a plate and put it down in front of Ursula. "Ian and Jamie are coming for the weekend," she said.

"Oh!" said Ursula, gazing at her aunt in dismay. The weekend was

ruined. Her cousins Ian and Jamie were awful. Especially Ian, who teased her all the time and called her a baby, just because she loved dear old Fredbear with his bald tummy and his one glass eye.

Ursula didn't feel hungry any more. She scowled down at her pancake. "Why didn't you tell me before?" she said.

"Aunt Maggie only phoned last night," said Aunt Prudence. "She and Uncle Andy have to go up to town, and they're dropping the boys off on the way."

A car horn tooted outside the house. Aunt Prudence looked at the clock.

"That'll be them now," she said,

going to the door.

Ursula dashed out of the kitchen and raced upstairs. She had to hide Fredbear before that horrible Ian got his hands on him. Ian had once tied Fredbear to a stake and tried to set fire to him. She must make sure that nothing like that happened this time.

Ursula heard voices in the hall and feet on the stairs. She grabbed Fredbear, pushed him hurriedly into bed and covered him with the blankets. Then a noise behind her

made her turn round. Ian was
standing in the doorway.

"Come on, Ursula," he said.
"Let's have breakfast. Aunt
Prudence says we can go for a
picnic later on."

Had he seen, or hadn't he?

Ursula didn't know. All she could
do was keep her fingers crossed as
she followed her cousin downstairs.

Chapter Two

Ian and Jamie thought that Ursula
was just an ordinary girl, but she had
a secret that even Aunt Prudence
didn't know about. Ursula could
turn herself into a bear.

It was very simple. Ursula had
found the magic spell in a book in
the library. All she needed were a
few magic words, and a currant bun,
stuffed with a mixture of porridge
oats and honey. Ursula had tried it
and the spell really worked. She

could turn herself into a bear
whenever she liked, and a beefburger
and chips turned her into a girl again
every time.

Ursula found that turning into a
bear could be very useful sometimes,
and she always liked to have the
right sort of currant bun with her
everywhere she went. That was why
she put one in her rucksack later that
morning, before setting off for a
picnic with Ian and Jamie.

"Now, have you got enough food?"
said Aunt Prudence, helping them on
with their rucksacks.

"I think so, thanks," grinned Ian.
"Egg and tomato sandwiches,
smokey bacon crisps, an apple and a
carton of orange juice. Oh, yes. And

a carrot each, because it's good for our teeth."

"Hee-haw!" bellowed Jamie, galloping away down the street. Ian laughed and ran off after his brother.

Ursula stared as she watched them go. Ian's rucksack was stuffed so full it was almost bursting. It couldn't all be food. There was something else in that rucksack, and Ursula wondered what it could be . . .

She sighed and followed the two boys down the hill towards the river. She wished she didn't have to go, but soon the fresh air and the sunshine made her feel better. By the time they reached the bridge she was feeling more cheerful.

She didn't stay cheerful for long.

Ian and Jamie stopped to look down into the river, waiting for her to catch up. Ursula stood beside them on the bridge, and all three gazed down at the rushing water.

Ian took off his rucksack and unfastened the strap.

"I wonder if this stupid old teddy can swim," he said to Jamie. And out of the rucksack he pulled a very squashed-looking Fredbear.

"IAN! NO!" shouted Ursula, as he dangled Fredbear over the rail by one foot. Jamie made a grab.

"Let me do it, Ian," he said, pulling at his brother's arm. "I want to chuck him in."

Ursula watched in horror as the two boys pulled Fredbear in opposite

directions as if he were the rope in a tug-of-war. She never found out exactly how it happened, or whether they really meant to drop Fredbear off the bridge. But before she could do anything to stop them, both boys suddenly let go at the same time. Fredbear fell into the river with a splash.

"Oh dear. What a shame," said Ian.

Chapter Three

Ursula blinked back the tears as she
saw the river carry Fredbear quickly
away downstream. Crying wouldn't
do any good, she told herself sternly.
The important thing was to get
Fredbear out, before the water
soaked into his fur and made him
sink. But how was she going to do
that, when she couldn't even swim?

Pausing only long enough to give
Ian a kick on the shin, Ursula
hurried down from the bridge and

began to run along the river bank.

"Ursula! Come back!" shouted
Ian, waving his arms and looking
worried.

Ursula took no notice. She had
just spotted Fredbear, in his bright
yellow jumper, being swept around a
bend in the river. She must keep him

in sight, or he would be lost for ever.

On and on ran Ursula, and soon she had left the town behind. The river began to wind its way through fields and woods, and there was nobody about except a few fishermen. The stream was wider here, and not so fast. Ursula was able to slow down to a walk, and still keep Fredbear's bobbing yellow jumper in view. Now was her chance.

She looked around to make sure

she was quite alone.

"I know *I* can't swim," said Ursula. "But Ursula Bear can!" And without wasting any more time she pulled off her rucksack, unpacked the currant bun and took a bite.

"I'M A BEAR, I'M A BEAR, I'M A BEAR," chanted Ursula, chewing the bun as she hurried along. "I'M A BEAR, I'M A BEAR, I'M A BEAR."

A few minutes later, Ursula had disappeared, and a small brown bear was scampering along the river bank on furry feet. The magic had worked, and once again she had turned into Ursula Bear.

Fredbear's yellow jumper was looking dangerously low in the water.

Ursula flung the rucksack into some
bushes and dived into the river,
making a splash which set all the
ducks quacking in alarm. She swam
strongly out into the stream, and
soon she had a paw firmly round
Fredbear's soggy middle.

Turning towards the bank, Ursula struggled to get Fredbear back to land. But the river was getting narrow again, the water swept her along, and a loud roaring noise filled her ears.

Suddenly she saw a big red-painted notice sticking up out of the water.

"What's a weir, Fredbear?" she said. Fredbear either didn't know, or his mouth was too full of water to reply.

It wasn't long before they both found out.

Chapter Four

Ursula clung to Fredbear with all her
might as they went tumbling
together over the edge of the weir.
The sky vanished, the world went
black, water filled her eyes and her
ears, and for a long time she didn't
know which way was up and which
was down.

At last she was swept into calmer
water, and found to her relief that
she still had Fredbear clutched in her
paws. She took a great gulp of air,

glad to see blue sky again, and set off to swim for the shore.

Ursula was only a little way from the bank when she felt someone grab her by the shoulders, lift her out of the water, and set her on her feet on the grass. She stood there, dripping and staring, with Fredbear in her arms.

Her rescuer was a fisherman, wearing long green wellies past his knees and an old red jumper with holes in the elbows. He was staring at Ursula just as hard as she was staring at him.

"Good grief!" he said. "I don't believe this. A bear with a teddy? I'm seeing things!" Without waiting to pack up his fishing gear or his picnic basket, he turned and hurried away, muttering something about too much elderberry wine and sitting in the sun too long.

Ursula put Fredbear down in a patch of sunshine to dry. She was very glad that he was safe, but now she had a new problem. She had to

turn herself back into a girl again before she could go home, and there was no hope of finding beefburgers and chips on the river bank so far from the town.

She looked at the fisherman's lunch basket. There might be something in there which would do instead.

Ursula had to act quickly, for she knew the fisherman would be back before long.

"Sorry, fisherman," she said. "I wouldn't do this if I didn't have to." Then she opened the basket and put the contents one by one on the grass.

A bottle of home-made elderberry wine. A packet of sandwiches filled with something yellow and green that looked like mouldy cheese and smelled like it, too. A pork pie. Some chocolate biscuits. Another bottle of elderberry wine. Then, just as she was about to give up hope, she found something round wrapped in a plastic bag. It was a large bun, with sesame seeds on the top, and a big fat beefburger inside.

"Fredbear, look!" growled Ursula, jumping up and waving the beefburger in her paw.

Fredbear stared at the sky and said nothing. He didn't seem impressed at all.

Ursula sat down again with a bump. Fredbear was right. What was the use of a beefburger, without any chips?

Chapter Five

Carrying Fredbear and the
beefburger, Ursula trotted back
towards the town. It was nearly
lunch-time and the chip shop would
be open by now. Somehow she would
have to beg or steal a handful of
chips. Ursula didn't yet know how,
but she would worry about that
when she got there.

She hadn't gone very far when she
saw two girls coming towards her
along the bank and she scurried

quickly behind a tree until they had gone past. Then, as they came closer, Ursula stared hard at something they had in their hands. They were chatting and giggling as they walked along, and *eating chips out of paper bags with their fingers*.

"Chips!" said Ursula to herself. "What a bit of luck!" Then she dropped Fredbear and the beefburger and ran out from behind the tree. She scampered up to the girls and held up both her front paws.

"Please can I have some chips?" was what she meant to say, but in her growly bear's voice it didn't sound like that at all. All that came out was a fierce sort of "Grrrrrrr!"

The two girls almost jumped out of
their plimsolls in fright.

"Help! It's a bear!" cried one.

"It's going to bite us!" shouted the
other. They both flung their bags of
chips into the river and fled.

For the second time that day
Ursula had to go swimming, and
this time it wasn't to save Fredbear.
It was to rescue a couple of soggy
bags of chips which were rapidly
soaking up the water and beginning
to sink.

Ursula hurriedly dived in and
made a grab, but she was too late.

The ducks had beaten her to it. Quacking and squabbling and pecking at each other, they had torn the paper to shreds and gobbled up the chips before you could say tomato sauce.

"Greedy things!" said Ursula, as she climbed out onto the bank, empty-handed. Picking up Fredbear and the beefburger once more, she plodded off again towards the town, with water squelching out of her feet at every step.

She glanced about her as she went along, and after a while she recognised the place where she had dumped her rucksack. She poked about among the brambles, and there it was, safe and sound. It was only when she was pulling the strap onto her shoulder that she suddenly remembered what was in it. Egg and tomato sandwiches, orange juice, an apple, a carrot, and *a packet of smokey bacon crisps*.

Ursula opened the rucksack and stared at the crisps. "I wonder if they would work instead of chips," she said, turning them over in her paw. Crisps were only fried potatoes, after all. She decided it was worth a try.

Ursula hid among the brambles

and began to eat the beefburger and crisps, not forgetting to say the spell backwards as she munched.

"RAEB A M'I, RAEB A M'I, RAEB A M'I," she growled. "RAEB A M'I, RAEB A M'I, RAEB A M'I."

Two minutes later the little brown bear had vanished. The crisps had done the trick. Ursula was herself again, and feeling very pleased about it, too.

Chapter Six

The magic had worked just in time. No sooner had Ursula set off for home than she saw someone hurrying anxiously towards her along the bank. It was Aunt Prudence, still in her apron and her old slippers, and with her hair tumbling down around her ears. Trailing along behind her, looking shamefaced and sorry for themselves, were Ian and Jamie.

"Ursula! Thank goodness I've

found you!" cried Aunt Prudence when she saw her. "Are you all right?"

"I'm fine," said Ursula, hugging her aunt. Aunt Prudence plonked herself down on the grass to get her breath back.

"I couldn't make any sense of Ian's story," she puffed, mopping her hot face with her hanky. "Fredbear fell in the river . . . you ran off to try and save him . . . Ian and Jamie couldn't find you anywhere. At least they had the sense to come and fetch me."

Then Aunt Prudence noticed Fredbear, still in Ursula's arms and looking very damp.

"You've got Fredbear!" she said.

"However did you save him?" She stared at Ursula in horror. "I hope to goodness you didn't jump in!"

Ursula gazed at her aunt, thinking hard. She didn't want to tell fibs. On the other hand Aunt Prudence would never believe what really happened. She looked at her two cousins, who were staring at Fredbear in complete astonishment. They must never learn the true story, either.

"A fisherman got him out," she said at last. That was the truth, even though it wasn't quite the whole truth.

Aunt Prudence smiled, pleased that everything had turned out so well. She got up and brushed bits of grass from her apron.

"That was very kind of him," she said. "I hope you thanked him nicely, Ursula?"

Ursula remembered the fisherman waddling away in his wellies. She burst out laughing.

"I didn't get a chance to," she said. "He didn't seem to like bears much. Silly man!"

Ursula kissed Fredbear's damp nose and carried him off home before he caught a bad cold.